Adapted from *A Christmas Carol* by Charles Dickens
Retold by Sarah Powell
Illustrated by Louise Pigott

© 2017 Studio Press

Edited by Gemma Cooper • Designed by Rob Ward
Consultant Cindy Sughrue, Charles Dickens Museum, London
www.dickensmuseum.com

Printed and bound in China, 0240717
10 9 8 7 6 5 4 3 2 1

Studio Press
An imprint of Kings Road Publishing
Part of Bonnier Publishing
The Plaza, 535 King's Road,
London, SW10 0SZ
www.studiopressbooks.co.uk
www.bonnierpublishing.co.uk

A Christmas Carol

A Search & Find Book

Illustrated by Louise Pigott
Original Story by Charles Dickens • Retold by Sarah Powell

With an introduction by Cindy Sughrue, Charles Dickens Museum, London

Charles Dickens
1812-1870

Charles Dickens is one of the world's greatest storytellers. He was born in Portsmouth, England, in 1812 where his father worked for the Navy. His family moved a lot with his father's work, but finally settled in London when Charles was nine years old.

His family did not have much money, and his father had a habit of spending more than they had. He was thrown in prison for debt when Charles was 12. Charles had to go to work in a rat-infested factory to support his mother and four siblings, but the work didn't pay well. The family was desperately poor. When his father's debts were finally paid off, Charles was able to go back to school, but he never forgot the terrible experience of the factory and not having enough money. He was determined to work hard and make a better life for himself.

When Charles left school, his first job was as a clerk in a solicitor's office. He then went on to become a newspaper reporter and, when he realised he was good at it, he also started writing short stories and then novels. Many of these – like *Oliver Twist* and *A Christmas Carol* – were so popular that they were translated into other languages. Charles Dickens became famous all over the world and travelled to America and Europe. He also loved performing and gave dramatic readings of his own stories.

Charles Dickens died in 1870. He is buried at Westminster Abbey in London.

A Christmas Carol
1843

A Christmas Carol was Charles Dickens' first and best-loved Christmas book. It was an instant success when it was published in December 1843 and has remained extremely popular ever since. It has been made into plays, musicals, films, television programmes, cartoons, comics, ballets and operas.

Dickens experienced poverty as a child and wrote about this and other social issues that affected many people at the time. He believed that more should be done to help poor people and that everyone could make a difference by being more caring and generous.

A Christmas Carol is about Ebenezer Scrooge, a rich, mean and selfish old man who cares about no one and nothing except money. On Christmas Eve, he is visited by the ghost of his miserable former business partner, Jacob Marley, who warns him to change his ways before Scrooge ends up like Marley, roaming the earth in chains, tormented by the bad things he did when he was alive.

During the night, Scrooge is haunted by three ghosts: the first reminds him about his happier past, the second takes him to see how the people he knows are celebrating Christmas, and the third ghost shows Scrooge what will happen if he continues on without showing kindness and generosity to those around him. Scrooge is deeply upset by what he sees and begs the final ghost to let the future be different. Scrooge promises to be a better person. Dickens' story reminds us that it is never too late to change.

Cindy Sughrue, Charles Dickens Museum, London

Meet the Characters

There is a magical world of characters waiting to be discovered on the search and find pages. From the mean-spirited Mr. Scrooge and his clerk Bob Cratchit to the three Ghosts, Tiny Tim and Jacob Marley.

EBENEZER SCROOGE

"I will honour Christmas in my heart, and try to keep it all the year. I will live in the Past, the Present, and the Future. The Spirits of all Three shall strive within me. I will not shut out the lessons that they teach!"

FANNY SCROOGE

YOUNG EBENEZER SCROOGE

FRED

BOB CRATCHIT

MRS. CRATCHIT

TINY TIM

"It is required of every man," the Ghost returned, "that the spirit within him should walk abroad among his fellow men, and travel far and wide; and, if that spirit goes not forth in life, it is condemned to do so after death."

GHOST OF
CHRISTMAS PAST

GHOST OF
CHRISTMAS PRESENT

GHOST OF CHRISTMAS
YET TO COME

JACOB MARLEY

GHOST OF JACOB MARLEY

MR. FEZZIWIG

MRS. FEZZIWIG

THREE MISS FEZZIWIGS

Welcome to London

Where we meet …

Ebenezer Scrooge counting his money,
Bob Cratchit, overworked and underpaid,
Fred dutifully visiting his uncle, Scrooge,
Mrs. Dilber fetching Scrooge's laundry,
Tiny Tim, unwell but smiling,
Martha Cratchit working in a hat shop,
Mrs. Cratchit cooking for her family, and
Jacob Marley, who is very deceased.

Search and find:

*EBENEZER
SCROOGE*

*BOB
CRATCHIT*

*GHOST OF
JACOB MARLEY*

*FRED, SCROOGE'S
NEPHEW*

*MRS. DILBER,
A LAUNDRESS*

*SCROOGE'S
HOME*

*THE CRATCHITS'
HOME*

*MARTHA CRATCHIT,
BOB'S DAUGHTER*

*TINY TIM, BOB'S
YOUNGEST SON*

*MRS. CRATCHIT,
BOB'S WIFE*

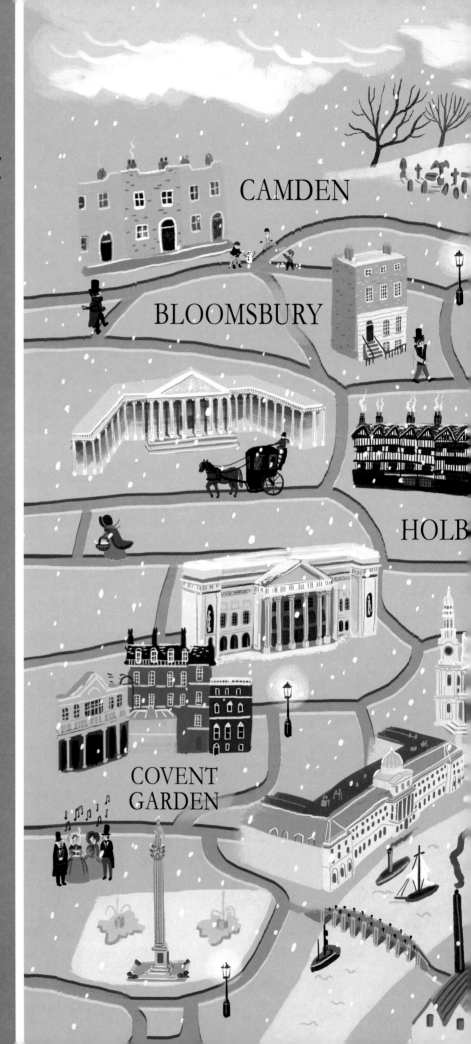

CAMDEN

BLOOMSBURY

HOLB

COVENT
GARDEN

CLERKENWELL

HOXTON

THE CITY of LONDON

RIVER THAMES

The Day Before Christmas

In which …

Scrooge proclaims his hatred of Christmas,
Bob Cratchit shivers in the cold office,
Fred arrives with an offer for his uncle,
Scrooge refuses Fred's Christmas invitation,
Charity collectors arrive asking for money,
Scrooge angrily denounces helping the poor,
Bob Cratchit runs home to his family, and
Scrooge grudgingly leaves for his house.

Search and find:

A HUMBUG SCROOGE

A BUSY BOB CRATCHIT

ONE BURNING COAL

TWO CHARITY COLLECTORS

A QUILL AND AN INKWELL

A CHEERFUL FRED

A BOY SELLING CAKES

A PORTRAIT OF JACOB MARLEY

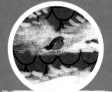

FIVE RED ROBINS

TEN SPRIGS OF HOLLY

The Ghost of Jacob Marley

In which …

Scrooge's sight plays tricks on him,
The door knocker seems to change shape,
The house is empty, dark and quiet,
Scrooge hears a dreadful moaning,
Marley's ghost appears to Scrooge,
The ghost brings a terrible warning,
Scrooge must change his mean ways, and
Three Ghosts will visit him that night.

Search and find:

*A SHOCKED
SCROOGE*

*A HAUNTED
DOOR KNOCKER*

*GHOST OF
JACOB MARLEY*

*A BOWL
OF GRUEL*

*A RINGING
BELL*

*A GRANDFATHER
CLOCK*

*GHOST OF
CHRISTMAS PAST*

*GHOST OF
CHRISTMAS PRESENT*

*GHOST OF CHRISTMAS
YET TO COME*

*TWELVE GHOSTLY
PADLOCKS*

The Ghost of Christmas Past

In which …

The grandfather clock strikes one,
A strange spectre appears in the room,
The Ghost shows Scrooge his past,
It's Christmastime at his childhood school,
Young Scrooge is alone every Christmas,
His sister Fanny arrives unannounced,
She is taking him home for Christmas, and
He will not be alone anymore.

Search and find:

A WISTFUL SCROOGE

A YOUNG EBENEZER SCROOGE

GHOST OF CHRISTMAS PAST

A HURRYING FANNY SCROOGE

A BUSY SCHOOL MASTER

A CHIMING SCHOOL BELL

A FROSTY WEATHER VANE

A FORGOTTEN SCHOOLBOOK

A RUNAWAY PONY

SIXTEEN HEAVY TRUNKS

The Fezziwig Party

In which …

Scrooge visits another past memory,
Mr. Fezziwig's party is in full swing,
Young Scrooge is treated like a son,
He appears happy and in love,
He dances all night with the lovely Belle,
Scrooge thinks of the poor Cratchits,
He regrets being such a humbug, and
Scrooge vows to be kinder to Bob Cratchit.

Search and find:

A THOUGHTFUL
SCROOGE

A YOUNG EBENEZER
SCROOGE

GHOST OF
CHRISTMAS PAST

A HAPPY
MR. FEZZIWIG

A LAUGHING
MRS. FEZZIWIG

A BLUSHING
BELLE

THE THREE
MISS FEZZIWIGS

A TUNEFUL
FIDDLER

A GREEDY
DOG

TWENTY
MINCE PIES

The Ghost of Christmas Present

In which …

Scrooge wakes up suddenly in his bed,
He wonders if the Ghost was a dream,
The Ghost of Christmas Present appears,
Scrooge's dark, cold house is transformed,
There's candlelight and a feast for a king,
The Ghost wears a magical green robe,
Scrooge is ordered to touch the robe, and
The Ghost and Scrooge disappear.

Search and find:

*A SURPRISED
SCROOGE*

*THE GHOST OF
CHRISTMAS PRESENT*

*SIX CHRISTMAS
WREATHS*

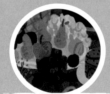

*TWELVE RED
APPLES*

*A SHINING
TORCH*

*THREE STRINGS
OF SAUSAGES*

*FIVE COOKED
GEESE*

*FOUR ROASTED
TURKEYS*

*A BOWL
OF PUNCH*

*FIVE TWELFTH
CAKES*

The City at Christmas

In which ...

Scrooge and the Ghost explore London,
They fly over the snowy rooftops,
They wander down frozen alleyways,
Chestnuts roast and carolers sing,
Everyone in London is happy,
The Ghost sprinkles blessings to all,
People celebrate on every street, and
Scrooge's once-cold heart grows warm.

Search and find:

*A FESTIVE
SCROOGE*

*GHOST OF
CHRISTMAS PRESENT*

*A GRINNING
GROCER*

*A HORSE
AND CART*

*A SPRIG OF
MISTLETOE*

*A NAUGHTY
CHILD*

*A PROUD
BUTCHER*

*TEN
SNOWBALLS*

*A SMALL
SNOWMAN*

*FIVE
HANDBASKETS*

The Visit to the Cratchits

In which …

Scrooge and the Ghost visit a small house,
The Cratchits are celebrating Christmas,
Mrs. Cratchit is busy cooking dinner,
Bob smiles at his wife and children,
Scrooge sees how poor the Cratchits are,
He realises how little they have,
Scrooge sees how sick Tiny Tim is, and
Scrooge begins to fear the future.

Search and find:

*A WORRIED
SCROOGE*

*FIVE GLOWING
CANDLES*

*A SILHOUETTE OF
BOB CRATCHIT*

*A CARRIAGE
CLOCK*

*A BONE FOR
A HUNGRY DOG*

*A SICK
TINY TIM*

*FIFTEEN
PLATES*

*FIVE
CARROTS*

*A CHRISTMAS
PUDDING*

*A ROASTED
GOOSE*

The Christmas Party

In which …

The Ghost takes Scrooge to Fred's house,
Fred is hosting a Christmas party,
Guests dance and play jolly party games,
Christmas spirit and cheer fill the air,
Everyone asks about Scrooge,
Fred's wife thinks Scrooge is mean,
Fred feels sad for his lonely uncle, and
Scrooge wishes he were at the party.

Search and find:

A SAD SCROOGE

GHOST OF CHRISTMAS PRESENT

A JOLLY FRED

A LAUGHING HOSTESS

TWO DANCING CHILDREN

A BOOK OF CHRISTMAS MUSIC

A PLATE OF JIGGLY JELLY

A CURIOUS CAT

A PLAYFUL SPOTTY DOG

A DECK OF CARDS

The Third Ghost

In which …

The last ghost finally arrives,
It's the Ghost of Christmas Yet to Come,
Scrooge is terrified for his future,
Some bankers speak coldly of a death,
Mrs. Dilber rushes to a pawn shop,
She has stolen the dead man's possessions,
No one cares for the dead man, and
Scrooge wonders who has died.

Search and find:

A CURIOUS SCROOGE

GHOST OF CHRISTMAS YET TO COME

A GOSSIPING BANKER

A RUSHING MRS. DILBER

A MEAN OLD JOE

A GRUMPY CHARWOMAN

A DUTIFUL UNDERTAKER

OLD JOE'S PAWN SHOP

FOUR BUSY HORSES

A LONELY BEGGAR WOMAN

The Death of Scrooge

In which …

The Ghost takes Scrooge to a graveyard,
Scrooge sees a terrible gravestone,
He realises that he was the dead man,
Scrooge suddenly sees the Cratchits,
Bob and his family are distraught,
Scrooge learns that Tiny Tim has died,
He vows to help the Cratchits, and
Scrooge promises to change his ways.

Search and find:

A REPENTENT
SCROOGE

GHOST OF CHRISTMAS
YET TO COME

SCROOGE'S
GRAVESTONE

JACOB MARLEY'S
GRAVESTONE

TINY TIM'S
FUNERAL

A SOLITARY
CANDLE

FIVE STONE
ANGELS

FOUR CAWING
CROWS

A POSY
OF FLOWERS

A SCURRYING
MOUSE

The Morning of Christmas Day

In which ...

Scrooge wakes up and is happy to be alive,
The three Ghosts have disappeared,
Scrooge is back in the present,
He now understands Christmas,
Scrooge gives money to charity,
He plans a big surprise for Bob,
A turkey is ordered for the Cratchits, and
Scrooge is filled with Christmas cheer.

Search and find:

*A JOYFUL
SCROOGE*

*A HELPFUL
MRS. DILBER*

*A BUSY
ERRAND BOY*

*A SURPRISED
CAROLER*

*A POULTERER'S
SHOP*

*SIX GREEN
BOTTLES*

*A LOST
NIGHTCAP*

*TWO CHARITY
COLLECTORS*

*SEVEN RED
BOWS*

*FOURTEEN
NEW HATS*

HATTERS

APOTHECARY

GUMM'S CONFECTIONS

The Christmas Festivities

At which ...

Scrooge knocks on his nephew's door,
Fred greets Scrooge with open arms,
Scrooge wishes all a Merry Christmas,
People see how Scrooge has changed,
Scrooge sings carols with a smile,
He dances with a joyful heart,
Scrooge enjoys the wonderful party, and
He laughs for the first time in years.

Search and find:

A CHANGED
SCROOGE

A SURPRISED
FRED

TWO CHRISTMAS
WREATHS

AN ENORMOUS
TURKEY

TEN SMOKING
CHIMNEYS

A CHURCH
CLOCK

GHOST OF
CHRISTMAS PRESENT

A HAPPY
TINY TIM

ONE LARGE
PRESENT

FIVE
CANDELABRAS

The Changed Scrooge

In which …

Scrooge becomes a friend to all,
Fred is proud of his happy uncle Scrooge,
Scrooge gives Bob Cratchit a salary raise,
Scrooge helps the Cratchit family,
Tiny Tim grows healthy and strong,
Scrooge's heart is full of laughter,
He learns how to keep Christmas, and
Scrooge never sees the Ghosts again.

Search and find:

*A HAPPY
SCROOGE*

*GHOST OF
CHRISTMAS PAST*

*GHOST OF CHRISTMAS
PRESENT*

*GHOST OF CHRISTMAS
YET TO COME*

*A THRIVING
TINY TIM*

*A FESTIVE
FRED*

*A CANDY-STRIPED
PRESENT*

*A MIAOWING
CAT*

*A BUCKET FULL
OF COAL*

*A CHRISTMAS
STAR*

CAMDEN

CLERKENWELL

HOXTON

BLOOMSBURY

HOLBORN

THE CITY
of LONDON

COVENT
GARDEN

RIVER THAMES

THE DAY BEFORE CHRISTMAS

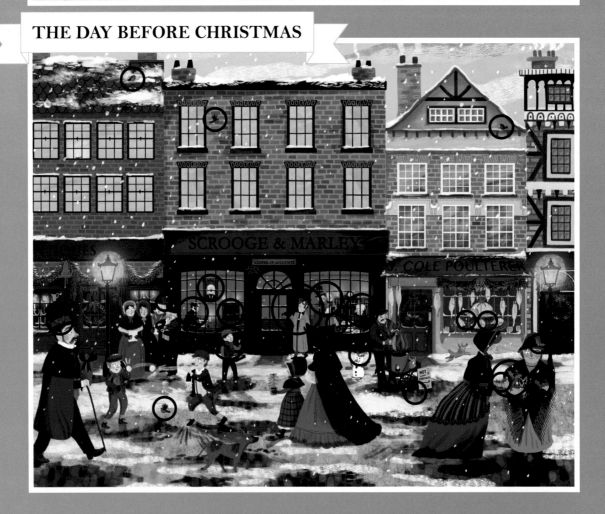

SCROOGE & MARLEY

KEEPER OF ACCOUNTS

J. COLE POULTERER

THE GHOST OF JACOB MARLEY

THE GHOST OF CHRISTMAS PAST

GROCER

THE DEATH OF SCROOGE

THE MORNING OF CHRISTMAS DAY

THE CHRISTMAS FESTIVITIES

THE CHANGED SCROOGE